Me and My
Flying Machine

ME and MY FLYING MACHINE

By MARIANNA and MERCER MAYER

Parents' Magazine Press/New York

*

To Peg and Dad

Last summer I discovered an old barn.
It was full of great things.

There were boxes, pieces of wood.
There were even nails and a hammer.
I could build anything I wanted.
I'll build a flying machine, I thought,
and I started building.
I worked all day.

My flying machine was almost finished
but it was dinner time and I had to
wash the dog.

So I closed up the barn for the night.
"Good-bye, flying machine. I'll finish you
tomorrow," I said and went home.

That night I dreamed about my flying machine
and how it would look when I was finished.
It would be something tremendous.
Smaller than a castle but bigger than a truck.

I finally decided on something smaller.
Besides, it would take me too long
to build a big flying machine.

There were so many things I could do.
I'd deliver mail to Eskimos and people
who never get mail.

I'd fly above the fog and rescue lost boats at sea.

I'd carry mountain climbers to the
mountain top. So they wouldn't have
to spend so much time climbing.

Birds could rest on the wings, if they
were tired from flying around all day.

From high in my flying machine I could see everything. So I'd always know where everything was and I'd never get lost.

I'd help cowboys catch their cows. After all, a flying machine is much faster than a horse.

My flying machine would win first prize in every race.

I'd do dangerous tricks in the air,
like hanging by my teeth
from a long rope, blindfolded.

And if I fell...

I wouldn't worry.
I'd just open my parachute
and drift safely down.

My flying machine would meet me when I landed.

And soon I'd have so many medals and
trophies that I wouldn't know where
to keep them.

I couldn't wait to finish
my flying machine.
The next day I ran all the way
to the old barn.

Everything was just like I left it.

There was more work to do so I nailed
on another wing and some stuff.

I finished working on my flying machine
but somehow it didn't look quite the way
I thought it would.

There was a brush and some old paint cans
lying around. So I used a little of each.
It was just what my flying machine needed.

It looked better than I had imagined.
So I tied a rope on the front end to pull
my flying machine outside to dry.

It creaked and moaned
and started to shake as I pulled.

And then before I could pull it out of
the barn...my flying machine
fell apart.

Tomorrow I'll build a rowboat.